John Birch

Examples of Stables, Hunting-Boxes, Kennels, Racing

Establishments, etc.

John Birch

Examples of Stables, Hunting-Boxes, Kennels, Racing Establishments, etc.

ISBN/EAN: 9783742810618

Manufactured in Europe, USA, Canada, Australia, Japa

Cover: Foto ©Andreas Hilbeck / pixelio.de

Manufactured and distributed by brebook publishing software
(www.brebook.com)

John Birch

Examples of Stables, Hunting-Boxes, Kennels, Racing Establishments, etc.

OF

Stables, Hunting-Boxes, Kennels, Racing Establishments, &c.

BY

JOHN BIRCH

ARCHITECT

AUTHOR OF 'DESIGNS FOR LABOURERS' COTTAGES,' TO WHICH WAS AWARDED THE MEDAL
AND PREMIUM OF THE SOCIETY OF ARTS, 'COUNTRY ARCHITECTURE,' 'STABLES
AND COUNTRY MANSIONS,' 'PICTURESQUE LODGES,' 'CONCRETE
BUILDINGS FOR LANDED ESTATES,' ETC.

WILLIAM BLACKWOOD AND SONS
EDINBURGH AND LONDON
MDCCCXCII

PREFACE.

A T the suggestion of my friends, and as a lover of the horse —one of the noblest, most useful, and perhaps the most abused animal of creation—I desire to place before my readers this little work, in the hope that these " Examples of Stables" may be considered worthy of emulation by some lovers of this animal desirous of seeing him properly housed and cared for ; and trust the hints and suggestions contained in this volume will be found generally useful to those requiring to build new stables, or who may have occasion to add to or remodel their present buildings. Many a one having to leave in great haste for the country, with little or no time to spare, has had good reason to be thankful for the speed of the thoroughbred, in not only reaching their railway station in time to catch their train, but oftentimes with a few minutes to the good. Such horses are frequently to be met with running in well-appointed hansom-cabs in this overgrown metropolis ; and this is, I fear, the ending of many a promising two-year-old reared for speed and not endurance.

I do not profess to have any knowledge of the veterinary surgeon's art, but I should very much like to see some really successful improvement in the way of horse-shoes. I consider there are good opportunities in this direction both in respect to the form of shoe and the method of shoeing.

We have not yet succeeded in finding a suitable description of street-paving calculated to afford a sound and good foothold for the animals, and at the same time durable and inexpensive. The shoes which are put on horses are made to obtain this kind of foothold ; but the shape and form of the shoe are never thought of in the construction of the upper surface of the road-way, and it is absurd thus to give a purchase to the animal in pulling his load without some suitable going for a good grip. The present street-paving is not at all satisfactory, and consequently nearly always more or less under repair. Had the same pains and expense been incurred in forming the old-fashioned granite roads as is now incurred in keeping the present wood-block paving in position, the result would have been much more satisfactory and much less expensive, as the first outlay would be the only expense attending it. I feel certain that the granite-paved road, on a hard Portland cement bed well laid to a good curve, would be much more durable, better for the horse's feet, and much cleaner for the foot-passenger, than any other kind which has since been devised. It would be a saving to the ratepayer, in this respect that repairs would be less frequent. The maintenance of our present system of paving forms a serious item, and anything likely to reduce the burden should not be thrown away.

Again, under the present condition of our streets at certain times in wet weather, it is quite impossible for a foot-passenger to pass along the populous thoroughfares without being be-spattered with mud of a very adhesive description. Such is not the case with stone-paving laid to proper falls, which is with every shower of rain washed clean. The wood-block paving and the asphalt now so much in use encourage the formation of this peculiar kind of mud, and a good shower of rain fails to remove it. Apart from this, the painful sights one meets with of poor brutes struggling under heavy burdens, straining themselves beyond their strength, is sufficient to justify complaints as to the unsatisfactory condition of our streets. The clattering of the hoof and noise of the wheels are quite as much felt on this material as on the granite. The latter well curved and not too closely fitted together on the upper surface, affords the horse a good foothold and going. He looks for a good grip on the hard ground quite as much as he does on the turf, and should he happen to fall, has some chance of getting on his legs again. I trust shortly some better plan will be devised for street-paving, affording greater cleanliness, less interruption in repairs, and in view of more humane treatment for the animal. The old roads such as the Romans made are preferable in every way to those now in favour. I am sure many who have some little acquaintance with this subject will agree with me.

I might now call attention to the stables in this large metropolis for the accommodation of omnibus and cab horses, and the like, as well as that of the humbler class, such as the small carmen, green-grocer, firewood purveyors, costermongers, and other small tradespeople struggling for existence. Large bus and cab companies must endeavour to pay as good dividends as possible, and frequently stables have to be provided in expensive localities not always where quiet can be had. Besides this, rents are so high, and consideration for the comfort of this poor creature so low in the greed of money-making, that not infrequently a horse has to breathe in one-third the space necessary for his wellbeing. What must be the condition of many of these stables towards the morning, not to speak of the overcrowding, defective drainage, insufficient and foul bedding, imperfect ventilation, and so forth ? No wonder there is such a consumption of horse-flesh, and the knacker prospers and can form himself into a company. The condition of the night cab-horse is a pitiable one. Any one might see this if he watched the mews in the vicinity of some square, say in the W. C. district, or some other locality at one time gay and fashionable. The poor wretch made the most of, with his hoofs blackened and his coat as bright as the wealth of the poor brute and his driver's pocket could afford to pay for, looks fairly well to the ordinary eye ; but on closer inspection, in many cases, his condition is not all satisfactory. Every artifice is used to deceive the authorities, who, unfortunately for the cause I am advocating, are much too easy and lenient in these matters.

Many a one rolling home at the small hours, or reaching a London terminus from the sister countries in the early morning, feels the advantage of a cab to reach his home. He seldom or never questions the condition of the animal attached to his conveyance so long as he gets to his abode ; yet in many cases the horse is only fit for night-work, and sometimes only for the knacker. I regret to say the majority of these animals have been well bred, and have known what it is to experience proper attention and kind treatment. Any one with some knowledge of the regimen observed in a racing-stable will know what a poor broken-down thoroughbred must suffer on night-work, dragging along a dilapidated four-wheeler ; yet every advantage is taken of their willingness for mercenary purposes, often driven until they drop dead, as the reader will have no doubt noticed. The cruel advantage taken of thoroughbreds, who will, under any conditions, go as long as their legs will carry them, is only akin to the rascally behaviour of the stableman at a country inn who robs your horse of his feed. Unfortunately this noble animal, so good and useful a servant, is the tool of jockeyism, and an instrument in the hands of filthy lucre.

Either the Society for the Prevention of Cruelty to Animals, or some other institution having for its object improving the condition of the animal, should take early steps for bringing about a better state of matters. I am sure many would feel only too pleased to subscribe to a fund for the passing of legal measures for the better housing and general welfare of this animal. With regard to the S.P.C.A., I would suggest giving money premiums at the end of each year to their officers, in proportion to the number of convictions attended by imprisonment or heavy fines. It may happen the officer may not appear in court to sustain the charge, although the witness is present and the case one of gross cruelty. Some inducement in this manner, by way of a prospective augmentation of income, might lead to an increase of vigilance, with much advantage to the poor quadruped. I am sorry to say that I fear some of these officers are not quite so zealous as the subscribers would wish, judging from the flagrant cases one sees. Generous assistance ought not to be withheld from a society of this kind, doing, as it is, all in its power. The claims of such institutions of a genuine description cannot be too strongly put forward in the interests of this animal, sent for our use and not to be abused, as we see them daily, which is a shame to this enlightened country.

I question very much whether the mode of housing horses in London has not had something to do with pink-eye. You cannot stable, say, ten or twelve horses in a cubic space only fit for five without injury to health. Overcrowding in the sleeping arrangements of the poorer classes of humanity,— the huddling together and want of fresh air,—induces fevers, a low state of the system, loss of energy, and general debility —all brought about by inhaling a poisonous atmosphere. If so with the human being, how much more so with the horse, who requires a much larger space in which to breathe than we do? There is great need for reform in this direction, and while considering the splendid prizes contended for on the turf, those in power and position might exert themselves a little to render the end of the horse somewhat more creditable to them than at present, and not allow our country to become as barbarous in this respect as some foreign countries one could name.

The present method of slaughtering horses is not, to my mind, a humane one. Only the other day a brutal exhibition of this kind took place in the street. Surely a poor animal so unlucky as to break his leg or thigh ought not to be left for hours in excruciating pain until the friendly knacker, licensed horse-slaughterer, or whatever he or his representative may be called, makes his appearance. Even then oftentimes he cannot put an end to the poor brute's sufferings without an exhibition of ignorance in his calling, which of all occupations ought to be carried out in a humane and speedy manner. Might not the police constable be provided with some means of humanely putting the animal out of pain, without waiting hours for the slaughterman? Some better arrangements ought to be made for accidents of this description, the results of which are so revolting. The knacker's trade in this extensive place is a lucrative one, and companies have been formed in this line of business, which I understand extends to many departments. London would appear to be its chief centre, as, besides the enormous consumption of horses which have lived here, consignments from the counties of Yorkshire, Lincolnshire, and elsewhere are sent by rail to London almost every night, and go as dead meat, I am told, provided one is slaughtered. This is all done during the night, when no society's officers are abroad. Why this should take place during the night I do not know, except perhaps to save expense and to obtain a better price for the animal alive than dead, or that a form of beastly cruelty may not be observed.

The laws concerning the transit and protection from unnecessary suffering of animals used for food are lax enough, and want serious alterations, as may have been noticed by any one who has travelled on the cattle-boats between Ireland and this country, say, from Waterford to Milford Haven. These poor animals reach Waterford by train, are taken through the cattle-yards, and from there to the boat; then they undergo a sea-passage, are disembarked, pass again through the yards, and are sent to their respective destinations by train or otherwise. To be considered fit for human food after passing through this is a question on which an eminent medical opinion would be of value.

I should much like to go on with the grievances of our friend the horse, but this hardly comes within the province of this little work, which is only designed to stimulate the erection of good stables, well planned and arranged, with some little attempt at scientific principles; but of this the reader may perhaps be able to judge. The work simply pretends to give a few examples and general suggestions for the arrangements of these buildings, without attempting any practical or theoretical phraseology. I daresay some may consider there is little scope for ingenuity or taste in the planning and arrangement of stables. Such has not been my experience, as good taste and ability can be brought to bear on this subject like all others when one applies himself to it, with the result that the latest improvements can be combined with taste, comfort, and economy.

In expressing the pleasure the preparation of this little work has given me, and in fondly cherishing the hope it may help to improve the condition and welfare of one of the noblest animals of God's creation, I have to acknowledge with many thanks the kind assistance I have received from my friend and countryman, Matthew Dawson, Esq., and from James Innes Murray, Esq., and G. S. Lowe, Esq.

JOHN BIRCH.

8 JOHN STREET, ADELPHI, LONDON, W.C.
February 12, 1892.

CONTENTS.

	PAGE	PLATE
INTRODUCTION,	15	
STABLE OFFICES ERECTED AT LAXTON, NOTTS,	29	I
STABLE OFFICES ERECTED AT UPTON, BERKS,	30	II
STABLE OFFICES ERECTED NEAR CHOBHAM, SURREY,	31	III
DESIGN FOR STABLE OFFICES FOR SEVEN HORSES, .	32	IV
VIEW OF THE STABLES AT RUFFORD ABBEY, NOTTS, AS RESTORED, . .	33	V
VIEW OF THE STABLES AT CIRENCESTER HOUSE, GLOUCESTERSHIRE,	34	VI
DESIGN FOR STABLE OFFICES FOR EIGHTEEN HORSES,	35	VII
DESIGN FOR STABLE OFFICES FOR TWENTY-THREE HORSES, .	36	VIII
STABLES ERECTED AT PARKSTONE, DORSETSHIRE, .	37	IX
DESIGN FOR STABLE OFFICES FOR TEN HORSES,	38	IXA
TRAINING ESTABLISHMENT, NEWMARKET, .	39	X
STABLES ERECTED AT GRAFTON HALL, CHESHIRE, .	40	XI
STABLES, PARK PLACE, SURREY, AS REMODELLED, .	41	XII
STABLES ERECTED AT WANDLE HOUSE, SURREY,	42	XIII
TRAINING ESTABLISHMENT, NEWMARKET, . .	43	XIV
DESIGN FOR STABLE OFFICES FOR SIXTEEN HORSES,	44	XV
DESIGN FOR STABLE OFFICES FOR FORTY-EIGHT HORSES,	45	XVI

c

	PAGE	PLATE
DESIGN FOR STABLE OFFICES FOR THIRTY-SIX HORSES,	46	XVI^A
THE STABLES ERECTED AT INGESTRE HALL, STAFFORDSHIRE—		
BIRD'S-EYE VIEW,	47	XVII
VIEW IN QUADRANGLE,	47	XVIII
VIEW IN QUADRANGLE,	47	XIX
EXAMPLE OF A HUNTING-BOX—		
VIEW FROM THE SOUTH-EAST,	48	XX
VIEW OF ENTRANCE FRONT, .	50	XXI
EXAMPLES OF HUNTING-KENNELS—		
PLAN A,	51	XXII
BIRD'S-EYE VIEW,	51	XXIII
PLAN B,	54	XXIV
BIRD'S-EYE VIEW, .	54	XXV
EXAMPLE OF LOOSE-BOXES FOR SUMMERING HORSES,	57	XXVI
EXAMPLE OF A HUNTING-STABLE—		
PLAN, .	59	XXVII
BIRD'S-EYE VIEW,	59	XXVIII
EXAMPLE OF A RACING ESTABLISHMENT—		
PLAN, .	61	XXIX
BIRD'S-EYE VIEW,	61	XXX

EXAMPLES OF STABLES, ETC.

W HEN, some forty years ago, the author used occasionally to spend his school holidays in the small village of Gullane, in the county of East-Lothian, not far from Edinburgh, where a few training establishments were then located, and in which he took a boyish interest, he little thought he would one day be called upon to design one of the largest and perhaps most complete set of stable offices that have been built during the present century, to say nothing of many other buildings he has designed and erected of a kindred character, or be connected in any way with horses or sport. At that time the l'Ansons had training-stables at this place before moving to Yorkshire, and trained for the late Mr James Merry of Belladrum, and others. The author can well remember the beautiful horse Chanticleer, and watching Macleod the animal-painter doing full justice to a portrait of the handsome grey.

The arrangement of the boxes in racing-stables in those days was somewhat after the present fashion, each being separated, although communicating with each other ; and if the author remembers aright, there was a good arrangement for lads' rooms, mess-rooms, saddlerooms, fodder-stores, &c. ; and the trainers' houses were neat and comfortable, with tasteful gardens and very simple pleasing exteriors, to the walls of which clung the rose-tree and honeysuckle.

One or two of the most successful trainers of the present day at Newmarket trained horses in their early days at this place. At that time between this quiet little village and the coast of the Firth of Forth near North Berwick, there was a considerable range of downs with fine pure bracing air, somewhat like the air of Newmarket Heath, and fairly good exercising grounds ; but being so far removed from racing centres, few horses were trained here except for racing purposes in Scotland. On the links in those days the old Scottish game of golf, now so fashionable in the south, was a favourite pastime with the trainers, their patrons, and visitors. The author has often witnessed many a hard well-contested battle. He remembers William and Robert I'Anson, and other turf notables, enjoying this game, as healthful and invigorating as curling in winter, another favourite Scottish pastime.

Being on very friendly terms with the late Mr Henry Savile, and a frequent visitor at Rufford Abbey while rebuilding the stables and superintending other works on this extensive property, the author can well remember the great interest this gentleman took in all matters relating to the horse, and with what pleasure he would accompany his friends over his well-appointed stud-farm, show them his dapper little Cremorne, winner of the Derby, Parmesan, and other sires, also his beautiful stud of brood-mares with their colts and fillies. A quiet stroll over these paddocks on a beautiful May morning was most enjoyable, and not to be forgotten by any one having a love for the horse. Not less pleasant was it to be staying at this comfortable house during the hunting season, with a meet of the hounds in front of the old Abbey ; and if a hunting-man, to enjoy a good run in the vicinity of the Dukeries, or be fortunate enough to obtain a few days' shooting in the well-stocked preserves : these pleasures, and the genial manner of the host, are, I feel sure, in the remembrance of many besides myself. Mr Savile was a thorough sportsman in every sense, and a most amiable and accomplished gentleman. He enjoyed a fair share of success on the turf ; but during the latter part of his career he lacked the class of horses he used to have, when at Ascot in one year the greater part of the trophies fell to his share. Latterly his colours seldom came to the front in important races ; and he passed away much respected and deeply regretted by a large circle of friends and acquaintances.

The author has added to this little work some designs he made for a small training establishment at Newmarket, at the request of the late Lord Falmouth and his favourite jockey. The best-arranged stables in Newmarket were inspected, and all the recent improvements were noted and embraced in these designs. The circumscribed nature of the ground, and other surrounding circumstances, to some extent governed the arrangement, and prevented the buildings being so freely planned and arranged as they might have been. The plans were well considered, and no pains were spared to perfect and make them as complete as possible ; but some alterations and changes took place in the training arrangements shortly afterwards, and the building of this establishment fell through.

Enough, perhaps, has been said about bygone days. I shall be very pleased if these little reminiscences will stir up pleasant reflections in the memories of those who remember these times. The pleasures of our youth, when all appeared bright and glorious, have been the happiest times with most of us, and one may be pardoned for fondly dwelling on them and the good old days, which, I fear, are not destined to return to this country again.

The author now respectfully desires to make a few remarks on building stable offices. Besides possessing a really good and well-arranged plan, the stables ought to have some pretension to architectural taste, as they are frequently placed near the house ; and on a large property, where the owner is fond of horses, they form an important adjunct.

Stables ought not to be placed too near the house, and yet not too far removed to be inconvenient. In adding new stables to old mansions, the position would be governed by circumstances ; but in an entirely new building the author suggests their position being in the vicinity of the servants' offices, unless, of course, the nature of the ground, and the desire to obtain certain views of the surrounding scenery, render this impossible. There are no hard-and-fast lines where the stables should be placed. To be within easy reach of the mansion, not too obtrusively situated, and comfortably nestling in some convenient spot, to blend and group with the surrounding landscape, would appear to be all that could be desired. It is most important that the position ought to secure as much of the sunlight as possible, and, in fact, be bright and cheerful for both man and beast.

Sometimes stables may be so placed in connection with the mansion-house as to greatly enhance the picturesque appearance as seen from the garden front and terraces ; and when partially concealed by judicious planting the effect is good. They may be sometimes arranged to adjoin the kitchen-gardens, and so form proper fruit-walls on those sides favourable for the growth of fruit-trees and the position of vineries, and other buildings connected with the gardens.

In this small work the author's object has been to show in a very simple form how it is possible to make such a building as the stable a well-planned, comfortable, and pleasing adjunct to the property, whether of large or small pretensions.

The author gives examples of about twenty stables, ten of which have been executed in different parts of the country, and include the stables at Grafton Hall, Cheshire (Plate XI.), which are found convenient and suitable for a moderate establishment. The stables at Wandle House (Plate XIII.) are perhaps the most complete of their kind, and no expense has been spared by the owner to make them show-stables—a pleasure to himself and his visitors. There the long façade was somewhat difficult to treat; but the result has been successful, and the building forms a pleasing termination to the vista, and serves to screen from view the adjoining property.

The stables at Parkstone (Plate IX.) may be taken as another example of what can be done in making a structure of this kind pleasing and unobtrusive, and at the same time possessing some quaint originality of treatment. This building is purposely disposed of on the ground that the effect from the north or entrance front of the house should be quaint, and harmonises with the house, which has been designed in a similar style.

The view of the stables at Park Place, near Windsor Park (Plate XII.), is an instance of how an old and incongruous building may, with a little trouble and care, be made to harmonise with the mansion. The additions are not of importance; but changing the appearance of the old part required some skill, with the result that the whole agrees and harmonises with the house, and answers its purpose in all respects. It is not often possible to change the general appearance of a group of buildings; but this is a simple case in point, where the remodelling and alterations have been successfully attained at a very moderate expense.

The stables at Upton and Chobham (Plates II. and III.) are also similar examples in this direction, all intended to show that these buildings, which frequently have to find accommodation for very valuable animals, can be planned on the most approved and economical principles, and externally made pleasing and characteristic of the purposes to which the building is devoted.

The large stables at Ingestre Hall, which were designed and built under the author's supervision for the Earl of Shrewsbury and Talbot (see Plates XVII., XVIII., and XIX.), show what can be done on a large scale. These stables provide accommodation for between fifty and sixty horses, about half in stalls and the other half in loose-boxes, and are considered to be one of the most complete stables of modern times. These were designed in the Jacobean style, to harmonise with the Hall, which the author restored after the great fire which took place there some seven or eight years ago.

Of the unexecuted works or designs mentioned in this book, perhaps designs IV. and VII. may be worthy of consideration ; also designs IXA., XV., and XVIA., may be commended to the reader as well-digested plans possessing something more than the ordinary external appearance, together with a thoughtful and well-considered plan. Take for consideration the design, Plate VII., for eighteen horses. Here the buildings form three sides of a square, the stable-yard being enclosed in front by a handsome balustraded wall with carved stone entrance-piers and ornamental iron gates. The washing-place forms the central feature, with a prominent gable—a clock and quaintly formed bell-turret over it marking the centre of the building. The loose-box stables intended for hunters are arranged on the left of the washing-place, with the saddle-room and mess-room adjoining, also saddle and harness cleaning-rooms attached thereto. The carriage-horse and hack stable is on the right-hand side of the washing-place, with a sick-horse stable and harness-room adjoining. These departments are arranged in the most convenient order. The animals being first taken to the washing-place, where harness is removed, are cleaned, and afterwards taken to their respective stalls without again crossing the yard. A staircase is placed on each side of the yard, leading to groom's, coachman's, and helpers' rooms, which occupy part of the upper floor. The hay, straw, and corn lofts are over the stables, and a double coach-house on each side—one for the house, the other for visitors' vehicles, &c.—perfects this range of buildings, which may be accepted as a well-considered plan.

In the design IV., for seven horses, this idea is well conceived for a small establishment where there is no home-farm, and where the cow-houses, work-horse stable, piggery, poultry-house, &c., require to be combined with the stables. These conveniences, forming as it were a farmyard on a very small scale, are placed in the rear, having a separate approach,—the dung-court being accessible to both sets of stables, thus enabling the front yard of the stables to be always kept free from litter and nuisance of any kind. Here in this case the hay, straw, and corn are taken to the lofts over stables from the rear without having to come into the stable-yard. By this arrangement the stables are always kept clean and fit for the reception of visitors.

The author would also strongly commend to the reader's attention design Plate VIII., which has been well planned, and might be reduced and adapted to the requirements of a moderate establishment at very much less cost. This plan can be perfected and made to possess all the leading features of the best-digested examples in this work.

Plate XV. is another design with a convenient plan. The design would suit any Elizabethan or Tudor house. The centre feature forms a gable with saddle- and harness-room and helpers' sleeping-rooms over. From either side of this central feature the stables and loose-boxes radiate. The block forms three sides of a quadrangle joined at the angles by turret-staircases leading to coachman's and groom's rooms. Hay, straw, and corn lofts are placed over the stables. The general effect is after the fashion of Plate VII.

The stables for ten horses (Plate IXA.) is somewhat peculiar on plan, as will be seen from the bird's-eye view. The arrangements are somewhat similar to Plate XI., and is on a larger scale, and would make a suitable and convenient set of stables for a country mansion in the Old English or Tudor style of architecture, and would look very effective and picturesque in a shrubbery or in some thickly wooded part near the kitchen offices.

In point of economy perhaps Plate XVIA. would be the least expensive design in this work, having regard to the number of horses provided for. This idea, with its simplicity of form and other advantages, will no doubt commend itself to the notice of my readers. The plan is unique, and shows an arrangement of stables not often met with.

In the plan of hunting-stable (Plate XXVII.) it will be observed the range of loose-boxes for hunters resting is placed towards the south, with doors from each loose-box, with this advantage that these boxes would be useful for summering the hunters as well as resting them during the hunting season. In all other respects this plan has been devised to meet the requirements of a moderate-sized hunting-box.

The several amounts named as the costs of the executed works can be relied on as correct.

The estimates attached to the descriptions of the *designs*—not *executed* works—are approximate, based on the author's judgment, and would vary according to circumstances. The probable estimates, however, may be taken as tolerably correct, being based to a large extent on what the *executed* works in this book have actually cost.

In concluding my remarks on the various executed and unexecuted designs contained in this little work, I would now desire to invite the reader's attention to a few observations on the chief points to be attended to in the construction of good stable offices.

A gentleman has a perfect right to exercise his discretion about obtaining professional assistance in the building of his stables, or any other work he may as an amateur, with the assistance of a builder, consider himself capable of bringing to a successful completion. But in the first place, this is a penny-wise and pound-foolish game ; and in the second place, I can say from an experience of upwards of thirty years, during which I have had the pleasure of seeing the works of several amateurs, I must confess I was less or more disappointed with the results.

The remarks on the construction of stables and their fittings, &c., seem to me to be fully placed before the reader ; but although complete in themselves, they are not, nor did I ever intend them, for practical instructions sufficient to enable any one with a slight knowledge of building to carry them out himself. Too many cases have come under my notice in the course of my professional career, where attempts have been made with the object of effecting what seemed to be a small saving, by dispensing with professional advice, and which have turned out disastrously for the owner. I have also had instances where professional men have been called in to make good the ignorance of others, and the saving anticipated proved to be no saving at all, but a genuine loss. Only those who have had experience in these matters are qualified to deal with them ; and if there are instances of persons little acquainted with them who have, fortunately for themselves, succeeded in gaining their object, they are exceptions, and only serve to prove the rule.

Site.—First a site has to be chosen, and in the selection of this much care and judgment ought to be exercised : it should be within

d

a reasonable distance of the house, and, I would say, well sheltered from the north-east, and if possible with a background of trees or some such plantation ; and if the edifice could be so placed, at the end of an avenue near the mansion. If picturesquely designed, this structure, whether on a large or small scale, might be made a very pleasing termination to the vista. Certainly the natural advantages of the situation ought to be studied and taken into account. In some successful landscape-drawings no buildings are shown. I regret this from an artistic point of view, as in my opinion the happiest water-colour is an example of rural life pure and simple, with the humble house adorned by nature only. Nothing can surpass it. When in its wildest and uncultured form, if I may be permitted to use the expression, it is in many instances far more beautiful than any works we can create or depict from imagination. Some may say, Look at Savernake Forest in Wiltshire, Oakley Park in Gloucestershire, and a few other examples of note, chiefly the works of the landscape-artist Brown, better known as "Capability Brown." I grant these are all good in their way ; but I contend that nature in its simplicity, or if I may say, in its wild and crude state, has more charms for me. The wildest and most unfrequented parts of our country possess a beauty far beyond any work in which the hand of man attempts to attain what we consider a standard of perfection, if there be such a standard.

To go back to the question under consideration—namely, the site. This should be as high and dry as possible, with the ground gradually falling away from it, and not situated in a swamp, where we find some buildings placed. The whole site to be covered by the structure should be cleared of all garden-mould to at least twelve inches below ground-line ; it should then receive a good solid stratum of dry brick or stone rubbish, not less than six inches thick, and above this a bed of Portland cement concrete six inches thick. You may be assured no damp will rise through this, and you will create a thoroughly sound and dry foundation upon which to raise your building.

Drainage.—The next important matter requiring consideration is the drainage. This should be as simple as possible, and free from complication ; the more simple it is, the more sure of success. Stables without drains are preferable, but in these much straw must be used to absorb the urine ; and really good ventilation is necessary to render the buildings sweet, pleasant, and free from ammonia. In loose-boxes and the like drains may be dispensed with, as it is possible to so lay the floors as to do without drains; but in ordinary stall or loose-box stables some kind of drainage is necessary. The usual iron channel-guttering should be avoided if one wishes a healthy and sweet stable. The automatic flushing-tank arrangement to be met with in some large stables is all very well so long as it continues in working order. Unfortunately this contrivance is more frequently in disuse than otherwise.

For the drainage of stables generally, the simple plan I adopted at Ingestre Hall stables, also at Wandle House stables and elsewhere, can hardly be improved on, which is to have one horse-pot in the centre of each box or stall, with the floor of box or stall falling to the pot each way. The pot should be one of the most approved description to check draught and counteract smell. From this pot, in each stall or box, a short piece of drain-pipe should be taken straight through the wall at the head of the box or stall, discharging into a small chamber outside the wall at head of box or stall, open at the top and communicating with what I call the outside drains. By this means the outside and inside drains are thoroughly disconnected, and any chance of effluvia from the outside drains prevented. Of course the drains should fall with the ground to a desirable point, and the urine might be conserved in a tank for farming purposes.

Water.—In our domestic buildings, as well as the stables, good water is of the greatest importance, and especially so for horses. Oftentimes spring-water is very hard, and impregnated with chalk or other matter injurious to both man and beast. The question of drinking-water is of the utmost importance if one wishes to keep either themselves, their servants, or animals in good health. So far as a stable is concerned, where a well might be sunk or town water obtained, I would arrange that this should be used solely for cleaning purposes; and for the drinking-water I would conserve every drop of rain-water from the roofs of the building, and convey it to a large underground tank suitable to the size of the edifice, and would cause all the rain-water to first pass through a small filter-tank charged with gravel, fine sand, and charcoal, capable of being easily cleansed and renewed as occasion required. The pump for the drinking-water might be placed either within or without the stable, as might be most convenient. The pump for the water for cleaning purposes might be near the well, in the vicinity of the washing-place.

Ventilation.—Perhaps next to good drainage and drinking-water proper ventilation would come in order of consideration : it is a very great desideratum in all buildings, and one would expect so important an element of health would receive much more attention than it does. In my opinion, the simpler the principles on which the method of ventilation is arranged, the more likely to be successful. To keep your horses warm, comfortable, and free from draughts, the fresh air must come in above them, whether standing up or lying down ; and the simplest means of arranging this is to have the windows made in two halves, fixed at the necessary height from the floor, the upper part of the window to fall inwards to admit fresh air and exclude draught—this to work in connection with a similarly contrived arrangement of a ventilator on the other side of the stable or box, and opposite the window or fanlight over the stable door. A current of fresh air coming from these points, some 8 feet or so above floor-level, would exhaust the vitiated air, and force it upwards through the apertures in the ceiling to the extracting-chamber. By mechanical arrangements, such as used for vineries and the like, the openings for the admission of fresh air could be regulated at pleasure, and by a similar mechanical contrivance the exhaust ventilators in the ceilings might be under control ; and in fact the whole could be so arranged, that any particular temperature might be sustained if necessary.

Paving.—The paving of the floors in stables is a matter which cannot be passed over without some comment. The best and most durable floor now laid is composed of plain buff adamantine clinkers set on edge in cement on a concrete foundation of some 4 inches thick. The foundation should have a floated bed or smooth face to lay the clinkers on. Sometimes these are made with chamfered edges ; but this is much to be deprecated, as the urine lodges in the grooves which are formed by the joints, and although the clinkers themselves are non-absorbent and impervious to the effects of urine, yet the liquid forms a small pool in every joint, is not easily removed, and soon becomes stagnant, thereby helping to vitiate the air in the stables. Neither is it at all necessary for the horses to be able to secure such a foothold as these chamfered bricks were designed to give. The straw itself is quite sufficient to ensure this when laid on a level surface ; and as horses are usually tied up and stationary, these chamfered grooves are not in any way necessary except under special circumstances. The plain adamantine clinker is, as I have already said, the most perfect material for the floor of a stable, and should be laid with proper falls towards the horse-pot. The horse-pot and trap should be of a strong approved manufacture, trapped so as to prevent any draught passing into the stable under the horse, and from this trap a 4-inch drain-pipe should be taken outside the wall and made to discharge into an open trap. It is not, however, always convenient to lay such an expensive floor. A capital substitute is to be found in the blue Staffordshire brick, which being of a hard metallic nature, is, when set on edge, a most durable and effective floor, and is impervious to any evil effects caused by urine. The rotting and disintegration which sooner or later eat into the surface of plain brick floors, by the absorbing of urine, places this kind of material outside the class of really good work. Where, however, it is desirable for reasons of economy to have it laid in preference to other and more expensive ones, it should always be laid on the edge and on a sound concrete bed. For stables, loose-boxes, and coach-houses, an inexpensive and substantial floor of granitic concrete is much used, and is vastly superior to the usual Portland cement floor, which, however well laid, will certainly at one time or other scale off in pieces.

Fittings.—We come now to consider what class of fittings is most suitable to stables. Of this I may say at once that there are several classes, and what is suitable in one case will not always be so in another, as I shall endeavour to show. For instance, where economy has to be kept in view, and at the same time efficiency to be secured, such fittings as were put in the loose-boxes of stables at Park Place (Plate XII.) are perfect of their kind, and answer every purpose. In this instance the divisions are constructed of quartering, lined on each side with deal of sufficient thickness, and finished with a skirting of elm-wood at bottom, slightly raised off the surface of the floor, and capped on the top with an oak capping. The walls are lined to the same height with similar boarding. The mangers and racks are made of the same material, and the former lined with zinc. Here we have an example of the least expensive method of finishing loose-boxes ; and the stalls may be executed in a similar manner.

For stables of a better class, the ordinary iron fittings supplied by a few of the best manufacturers make a very good finish, combined with pitch-pine boarding stained and varnished. The ordinary iron fittings for manger, heel-post, ventilating rails, &c., should be of wrought iron in preference to cast, as the latter will not stand rough usage; and they should be of a plain, simple, and good character, without too much brass, which entails much labour in keeping bright. Whilst on this subject I may remark that it is a mistake to lay water on to the mangers; it is infinitely better to water the horses with iron pails from a tap in each stable.

The wood-lining to walls, and filling in of divisions for a really good stable, ought to be of oak or teak—the latter for preference. Elm is a very good material, and although not affected by the action of urine, is liable to warp and twist, and when used should always be tongued with iron. Where horses are given to kicking, the boarding should have strips of stout hoop-iron screwed on. All divisions should have the bottom rail raised off the floor so as to allow of proper cleaning and flushing, and for other reasons not necessary to mention. Where the boarding is placed against the walls, it is well to have the brick-work behind same rendered in cement. All protruding corners of wood-work likely to be gnawed by the horses should be plated with zinc. The iron fittings should be enamelled with hard and well-polished material, and even then care should be taken so to dry and ventilate the whole space that the enamel may not be discoloured by the steam from the horses, as is often the case. The space against the wall above the mangers should be tiled with tiles of a colour toned so as not to affect the eyesight of the horses—cinnamon, buff, or cream colour being preferable to white or blue; in fact, the latter should always be avoided. The same remark applies to the colouring of the walls above the boarding. They should, in good work, be finished with glazed bricks or polished cement. If done in glazed bricks, the walls could, with advantage and very little extra cost, be designed in panels formed with bands of coloured bricks, as was done at the stables at Wandle House (Plate XIII.) The walls of the cleaning-places should be of glazed bricks of suitable colour for the sake of cleanliness, and the same may be said of the walls in coach-houses. They do not harbour the dust so easily as plaster or cement, and the latter mode is liable to breakage and chipping, which becomes very unsightly.

Heating.—The necessity of heating the coach-houses is apparent, and the best method of doing so is by a small gas-furnace, with a flow and return pipe taken round the chamber. This arrangement requires no attention whatever beyond turning on the gas, and daily filling the cistern with a jug of water to make up loss from evaporation. Besides, there is no dust nor smoke to injure the carriages, as would be the case if coal-fuel was used. All that is required is to preserve the air within the chamber in a dry condition. Anything beyond this condition on the one hand, or approaching to damp on the other, is injurious to the construction and enamelling of the vehicles. This mode of heating was carried out at the stables last mentioned, and has been found to answer admirably.

Fireproof.—The floors over stables, coach-houses, &c., should always be made fireproof. It is but a small addition to the expense, and in a good stable should never be omitted. They may be formed of iron joists and cement concrete; and if the under part is smoothed and tinted French grey or salmon colour, and the iron joists chocolate or blue, the effect is very pleasing, and harmonises with the colour of the walls, and teak or other fittings.

Measuring-slides, &c.—Hay, straw, and corn shoots from the lofts over should be provided in each stable, with proper measuring-slides for one feed. The recesses in the windows should be utilised as cupboards for horse-combs, brushes, &c.; or benches may be made in them for sitting on, with hinged tops. This may be done in each alternate window, as found convenient and necessary.

· STABLE OFFICES · LAXTON · NOTTS ·

PLATE Nº 1

VIEW TOWARDS THE VICARAGE.

J. Akerman, Photo-lith, London

EXAMPLES OF STABLES.

PLATE I.

Stable Offices erected at Laxton, Notts.

THIS view shows the stable offices of a new vicarage built in
Notts. Besides the usual stable and coach-house accommodation, there is provision designed for groom, and a large space for
fodder, with access and provender-shoots. The cost has been under
£400.

This building is adapted for a small residence, such as a rectory,
shooting or hunting lodge, or small jointure-house, and would group
well with any house of picturesque design, contiguous or near to it.
The sky-line is broken by the ventilator, which, with the general
appearance, serves to indicate the purpose of the structure. The
courtyard is screened by a wall above the average height of a man,
so that all the grooming of the animals and other works pertaining
to the stables are hid from view,—a necessary precaution where
the stables form a feature in the landscape, as seen from the precincts
of the house.

The plan might be enlarged to obtain three stalls and one box, or
for a stable of two boxes and three stalls.

c

PLATE II.

Stable Offices erected at Upton, Berks.

THESE offices were erected near Didcot. There is accommodation for four horses, with all the other necessary accessories,
and lofts and grooms' rooms are provided for over same. The
building is of red brick, broken up with blue brick courses; the
roof is covered with red Staffordshire tiles. The main feature is
the stable, which is grouped in the centre, and a half-timber gable
projecting towards the courtyard, finished on top with a ventilator
and iron finial or weather-vane. The view given shows the picturesque
effect rather towards the court, as the building is designed to be apart
from the house, and the appearance towards the outside and back
not to be studied so much as towards the courtyard, the only place
into which visitors would enter. The site for such a building should
not be close to the mansion, but in the park, or nestling on the border
of a game-cover, or in some similar position near to it, not too far
removed from the house.

The cost was under £650, and this size of stable offices is suitable
for a country-house of some £4000 value.

STABLE OFFICES

VIEW IN STABLE COURT

STABLE OFFICES

··GUNNERS··

·NEAR· BAGSHOT·

PLATE Nº 5

VIEW LOOKING INTO YARD

J. Akerman, Reigate London

PLATE III.

Stable Offices erected near Chobham.

THIS drawing shows the offices of a picturesque red brick and half-timbered house near Chobham Common in Surrey. The entrance to the stable is in the centre, and marked by a gable thrown out over it. The stable is open to the roof, thus gaining all the available breathing-space for the animals that it is possible to get. The building is unpretentious, and the coach-house is built detached from the stables. Provender-lofts and grooms' rooms are provided, the latter being on the ground-floor. Red brick and tile roofing have been used in the construction, and the floors are of Portland cement concrete. The exterior aspect of the building is rendered picturesque and quaint, in so far as the ventilator, instead of being put over the centre, has been placed to one side, but directly over the stable, and a pleasing effect thus attained.

The cost of these offices has been about £750. This plan, with the addition of another building, say, to contain boxes for four hunters, and forming three sides of a quadrangle, occupying a position opposite the coach-house, might be built for about £1000.

PLATE IV.

Design for Stable Offices for Seven Horses.

THIS design is adapted for a small estate, and is an example of a symmetrical disposition of the parts of the plan. The form is one that adapts itself to the requirements very readily, and also lends a picturesque effect to the exterior of the building, of a character not to be found in the preceding Plates. The accommodation here is for seven horses; but, of course, the idea could be enlarged to provide for more, say ten or twelve horses. The grooms' and helpers' rooms, provender-lofts, &c., would, as in the previous examples, be over the stables, coach-house, and harness-room. The style chosen here is well adapted to stable offices and to a stone-producing country. The entrance to stables is again indicated by the arch, and a gable in the centre of fore-court, slightly elevated above the surrounding building, and crowned with the ventilator, forming an unmistakable feature in the open courtyard. Right and left are the mess-room and the coach-house, &c. The quadrangle is completed by a low enclosing wall, with gateway in front and tool-house and earth-closet at each angle. The introduction of quaint stone finials, stone copings, and lead lights in the windows, helps to produce an effect often attained in the examples of old buildings of this kind to be met with in such counties as Gloucestershire and others where stone is plentiful.

The cost would be about £1400.

The idea may be enlarged to provide for ten horses, at a cost of about £2000.

PLATE No 4

DESIGN for STABLE OFFICES

VIEW LOOKING INTO STABLE YARD

J. Akerman, Photo Lith London.

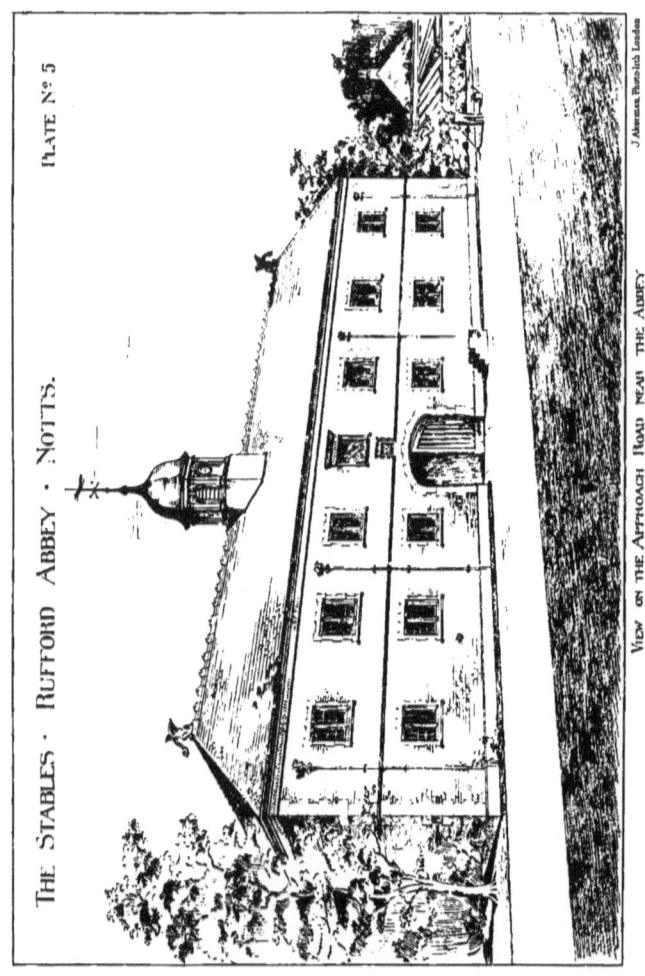

THE STABLES · RUFFORD ABBEY · NOTTS.

PLATE Nº 5

VIEW ON THE APPROACH ROAD NEAR THE ABBEY

J Akerman Photolith London

PLATE V.

View of the Stables, Rufford Abbey, Notts.

THIS drawing shows some old stables which the author partly restored for a gentleman in Nottinghamshire some time ago. The square form of this building is not favourable to any architectural effect, although some might prefer the simplicity of such a work. But the utter want of anything to relieve the monotony of the front, or any projection or irregularity of plan to produce the effect of light and shade, is an architectural defect at once to be detected, and certainly cannot be recommended in the construction of a new building. Being an old building, however, it was thought desirable to preserve its former character as much as possible. The stables were built in the reign of Henry VIII., and although the edifice seemed to have been fairly well cared for, it had gradually fallen into decay. There is accommodation for twenty-eight horses, and the quadrangle is entered by an archway on each of three sides. It is built of red brick and stone dressings.

34

PLATE VI.

View of the Stables at Cirencester House, Gloucestershire.

FITNESS, economy, and durability were the prevailing ideas in the conception of these stables, which the author rebuilt upon their old site for a nobleman in the West of England. These facts also account for the peculiar formation of the plan, which occupies one side of a large open courtyard. The walls are built of stone, and the roof covered with slates. The accommodation provided is for six horses and four carriages, mess and saddle rooms, coachman's residence, valets' rooms, hay and straw loft and granary, the latter being over the stables. There being no opportunity given to indulge in architectural fancy, the author has tried to make as simple a building as possible, having regard to the circumstances under which the works were executed, and has made no attempt to give importance to a building which otherwise has been found to give satisfaction in all its internal arrangements. The ventilator on the roof is made of oak.

THE STABLES · CIRENCESTER HOUSE · GLOUCESTERSHIRE

PLATE N° 6

VIEW IN THE COURT YARD

J. Akerman, Photo Lith London

DESIGN

STABLES for

EIGHTEEN HORSES

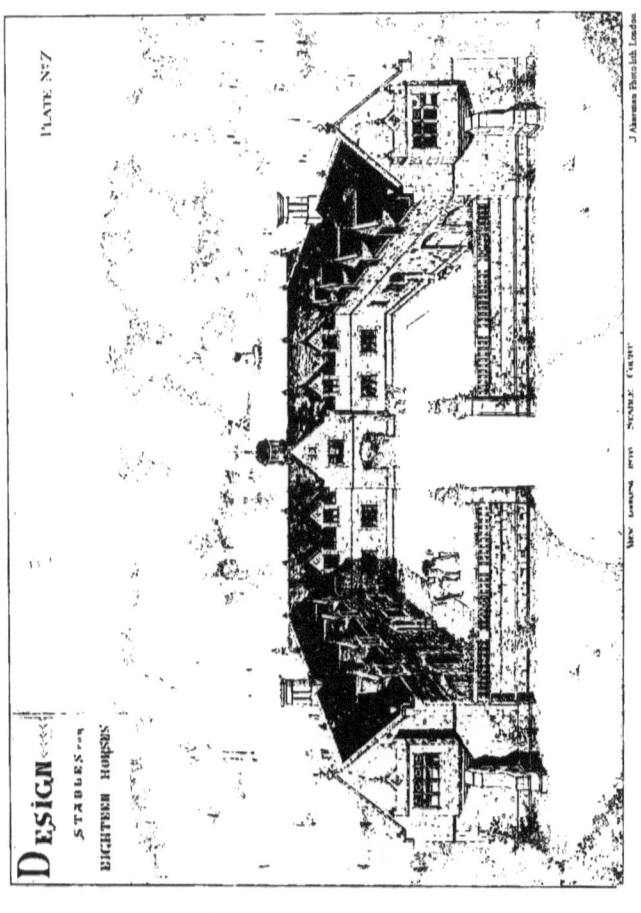

J Akerman Photo lith London

PLATE VII.

Design for Stable Offices for Eighteen Horses.

IN the planning of stable offices of any size, the form most to be recommended is the quadrangular. All the parts are brought together, and each opens out into the centre, and so much of time and trouble is saved in communicating from one place to another as cannot be obtained by any other form. The design shown in this drawing is planned upon this principle, and provides for eighteen horses, as well as accommodation for grooms, and other necessary adjuncts to the stable. Forming three sides of a quadrangle, and enclosed in the front by a low balustraded wall with gateway in centre, it claims somewhat more architectural pretension than the preceding designs. A stone-built structure, with a central feature surmounted by a bell-turret, the eaves on the three sides of square being broken by stone dormers, relieving the long stretch of roofing otherwise exposed, make up a harmonious and symmetrical design; while the gables of building immediately looking on to the park or stable approach are relieved by projecting windows of an ornamental character, which also serve to augment the size of the rooms which they light. This design would form a pleasing feature in an avenue to the north-east of the mansion.

The cost may be put at £4000. The style would harmonise with a Tudor, Elizabethan, or Jacobean house, but at the same time could be altered to suit circumstances.

PLATE VIII.

Design for Stable Offices for Twenty-three Horses.

THIS design is suitable for a large establishment, and provides for twenty-three horses. The buildings are quadrangular, and may be placed to the north-east of the mansion, on an approach-road to be used by tradesmen and domestics only. On the right side of the quadrangle are stables for carriage-horses and hacks, on the left is the hunting-stable, stable for sick horse, washing-place, harness and saddle room, and mess-room. Stall-stable, coach-house, harness-room, and washing-place are provided for on the other side of the quadrangle for visitors' horses, with a large dung-court in the rear. The coach-houses are on each side of the central archway, and rooms for grooms, coachmen, helpers, and valets, and also provender-lofts, are provided on the first floor, and approached by staircases on each side. A covered exercise-ground would be a great acquisition, and might be formed round the quadrangle with advantage.

The exterior has architectural pretensions, the principal entrance being marked by an imposing tower, with archway under, and the eaves are broken up by quaint dormers. To be seen at its best, a building of this size should be set back from the approach a full and liberal distance.

The probable expense of this building would be about £7500.

STABLES for a DUCAL MANSION

· VIEW OF STABLES LOOKING TOWARDS THE MANSION·

J. Akerman, Photo-lith. Prc-ca

STABLES · LILLIPUT · DORSETSHIRE

PLATE Nº 9

VIEW TOWARDS THE S·W·

J. Akerman Photo-lith London

PLATE IX.

Stables erected at Parkstone, Dorset.

THESE stables were designed and built by the author for a
gentleman in Dorsetshire, near Bournemouth. They afford
accommodation for three stalls, coach-house, coachman's residence,
and some smaller adjuncts. The structure is built of red brick with
hollow walls, half-timber and weather tile, and roofed with Broseley
tiles. The drawing shows the view as seen from the entrance to the
house on the north side. Entrance to the stable-court from the house
is through the archway between the two buildings. In the centre of
court is the coach-house and harness-room, and entrance to groom's
residence over, marked by a half-timber old-fashioned gable and
window and clock. On one side of the court is stable for three horses,
and on other side stable and coach-house for visitors' carriages, cart-
house, potting-shed, &c. The internal fittings are of a plain description; but the exterior is more or less elaborated, especially on the
side towards the house, as shown by the drawing. The effect is
enhanced by being broken up with deep projecting chimney-stacks,
and half-timber gable, and presents a picturesque and attractive appearance, looked at from all sides.

The cost of this building was under £850, and a more extensive
plan could be schemed on the same lines and with the same effect.

PLATE IX_A.

Design for Stable Offices for Ten Horses.

THE plan upon which this design is contrived was suggested by an ancient stable building in the midland counties. This building was constructed in the form of a crescent, which was considered as presenting all the fronts of the building free and open to the sun. Following this principle, I have adopted three sides of a hexagonal figure, as being an improvement on the other, and completing the figure by the fore-court enclosing walls. The accommodation is for ten horses, there being four loose-boxes and six stalls, and a proportionate amount of accommodation in respect of the other necessary requirements similar to the preceding plans. The animals are confined to the centre block in two stables, with a cleaning-place in the centre, and on each of the side-wings are the coach-house, harness, saddle, and mess rooms and accessories. The offices and dung-pit, &c., to the rear of the stables, are reached through the arches which connect the side-wings with the centre building, and also give access to paddock and fields beyond. The architectural features of this design are somewhat more elaborate than the preceding drawings show.

The cost of such a building would probably be about £2500.

STABLES FOR 10 HORSES

J Akerman Photo lith London

PLATE Nº 10

TRAINING ESTABLISHMENT · NEWMARKET

J. Ackermann, Photo lith. London

PLATE X.

Design for a Training Establishment at Newmarket.

THIS drawing shows a design for a training establishment intended
to have been built at Newmarket. The accommodation consists
of loose-boxes and stall-stables for sixteen horses, with provender-lofts
for these, harness and saddle rooms, coach-house and lads' rooms, also a
mess-room for the latter. The buildings were to adjoin the public road,
to be built of red brick, with stone dressings to doors and windows,
and tiled roof, with occasional half-timber projecting gables, and open
timber entrance-porch. The dwelling-house contains three reception
rooms, kitchen offices, and five bedrooms, bath, and w.-c., on the
chamber-floor. Access to the stable-yard from the house is provided
at the rear of the dwelling.

The probable cost of this building was estimated as under £3300,
and could be built on a larger or smaller scale if necessary.

PLATE XI.

Stable Offices erected at Grafton Hall, Cheshire.

THIS building was erected from designs by the author in the county of Cheshire. The form of plan decided on is ⸦-shaped, with a fore-court similar to Plate IV. The centre portion is occupied by stall-stable and loose-boxes, and affords accommodation for six horses. Coach-house, harness-room, mess-room, &c., are found on the ground-floor of the side-wings, and coachman's residence, valets' rooms, and straw-loft over. The entrance to the stables is through the archway and cleaning-place, and is marked by a gable, with an oak ventilator overhead. The walls are built of Runbon red bricks, and the roof covered with Staffordshire blue tiling, which makes a very pleasing combination. The dressings to doors and windows, &c., are of a reddish sandstone. All the floors are fire-proof, and the whole is built in a most substantial manner. The external treatment of the design was made to accord with the old house, the stables being placed at the east end, and contiguous to it. Quaint stone finials, and large chimney projections with angular shafts, harmonise with the surroundings. It was necessary, as the courtyard was near to, and visible from the house, to make the fore-court walls a convenient height, and at the same time give it some architectural character, in order to lighten the otherwise depressing effect of a blank wall.

There is also incorporated in this building, under the same roof, approached from the rear, a cart-horse stable and cow-house and shed.

This stable plan has answered admirably the purpose for which it was designed.

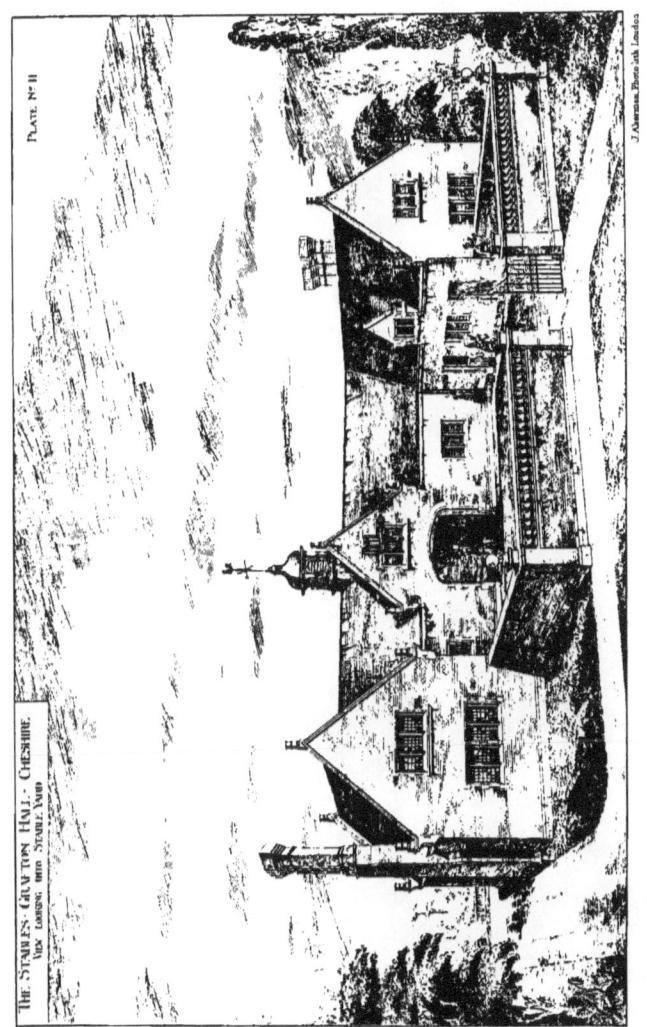

PLATE. Nº II.

THE STABLES. CREWE TON HALL. CHESHIRE.
VIEW LOOKING INTO STABLE YARD

J. Akerman. Photo-lith. London

VIEW IN THE STABLE COURT

PLATE XII.

Stable Offices, Park Place, Surrey, as remodelled and enlarged.

THIS building has recently been remodelled, and some small additions made by the author, and carried out by him as much on economical lines as efficiency would permit. The accommodation comprises two stalls and six loose-boxes, harness-room, coach-house for four carriages, coachman's residence, and provender-loft. The internal fittings of the loose-boxes are of a plain description, but sufficiently durable, and well adapted to the purpose, and the chambers are ventilated and drained on the latest improved principles. The floors are of Wilkinson's granitic paving, a comparatively inexpensive and durable floor, much used in military stabling.

PLATE XIII.

Stables erected at Wandle House, Surrey.

THIS view shows a departure in the general form of plan from the principles advocated in the preceding examples. The form of the site and other exigencies compelled the adoption of a long building; but although it is not a form to be recommended in the designing of stable offices, yet it has in this case been found to work very well. It provides for six horses in loose-boxes. These boxes are placed in one chamber with a lofty roof, and open from end to end; the walls being lined with the best quality of white glazed brick, with ornamental blue bands, presenting a very clean and handsome appearance. The fittings are of the best description, supplied by a well-known firm. The floors are laid with buff adamantine clinkers. Adjoining the stable is a spacious coach-house to take upwards of eight carriages. Harness-room, mess-room, cow-house, fodder-place, and other adjuncts are provided, and as each communicates with the other, the whole length of the building can be traversed without going outside. The building is of brick, cemented on the outside to imitate stone; the roof is slated. It is designed externally to harmonise with the house to which it is attached.

The unusual length of the building rendered it somewhat difficult of successful treatment externally; but the monotony that would otherwise have arisen is avoided by breaking up the front wall into bays, and marking the centre by a pedimented projection and large oak ventilator with clock-turret. Smaller ventilators are placed at intervals on the roof, and serve to break the sky-line.

The cost of this work was about £2300.

THE STABLES · WANDLE HOUSE · SURREY

VIEW FROM THE LAWN NEAR THE HOUSE

Plate No 14

A Bird's-eye View of Young Establishment Nazareth

J. Akerman, Photo-lith London

PLATE XIV.

Design for a Training Establishment at Newmarket.

THIS drawing shows a design for a training establishment at Newmarket, which the author was asked to prepare by a gentleman a few years ago. The building to the left side of the stable-yard contains accommodation for seven horses in boxes, and a spare box for a sick horse, and over these is placed the straw-loft, with suitable accesses. The wing on the right side provides for eight horses (making a total of fifteen horses), with lofts and lads' room over. The centre building consists of harness-room, coach-house, boiler-house, &c., with lads' rooms over; while a mess-room and coal-store is provided at the rear of dwelling-house. Dung-court and other conveniences are placed in the far corner of the stable-yard. The dwelling-house comprises three reception rooms and servants' offices on the ground-floor, and has five bedrooms on the chamber floor, besides a bath-room and w.c. The exterior is of brick, with cement dressings to doors, windows, &c., and the roofs are covered with red tiles.

The probable cost of this would be about £3000.

PLATE XV.

Design for Stable Offices for Sixteen Horses.

THE view given in Plate XV. is a design for a building in connection with a large estate. The provision is for sixteen horses. The form of plan adopted here is that of a central block and two side-wings, communicating with each other by the staircase turrets in corners, and making a quadrangle with fore-court walls. In the centre block are the loose-boxes and stall-stables, with lofts, &c., over them ; and on one side-wing the mess-room, harness-cleaning room, harness-room, and valets' rooms over are provided ; and on the opposite wing, coach-houses, sick-box, and coachmen's residence over. The fore-court wall has been designed low, as the architectural pretensions of the building and the spacious fore-court demand it. The tour of the building can be made without coming outside, which is a great advantage both to visitors and stablemen.

The walls are of red sandstone up to the first-floor level, and above that of red brick and stone dressings. The entrance to the court is in the centre, facing the principal feature in the quadrangle.

The cost of such a building would probably be about £3500.

PLATE No 15

SKETCH VIEW OF STABLES FOR 16 HORSES

VIEW LOOKING INTO STABLE YARD

DESIGN FOR STABLES FOR 48 HORSES

PLATE Nº 16

VIEW OF THE PRINCIPAL FAÇADE

J.Akerman.Photo lith London

PLATE XVI.

Design for Stable Offices for Forty-eight Horses.

THIS design is on a larger scale than any of the preceding, and more suitable to a princely establishment. The plan is conceived much upon the same principles as the others, the requirements being merely multiplied. The quadrangular form gives an opportunity for providing a glass-covered exercising space in the centre, which must be very essential where a numerous stud is kept. The courtyard is entered by an archway of noble dimensions in the centre of the façade, surmounted by a pediment with coat of arms carved on the tympanum, and a prominent clock and bell turret over, of oak and lead, high enough to be seen from all quarters.

The probable cost of executing this design would be about from £18,000 to £20,000.

PLATE XVIₐ.

Design for Stable Offices for Thirty-six Horses.

IN conceiving this design and adopting the form indicated by the drawing, the main object of the author is to arrive at a plan which will give the greatest accommodation consistent with economy of space ; and for a large establishment this form would doubtless work very well. On either side of the entrance, which is indicated by the archway and half-timber elevation over it, are to be found the coachmen's and grooms' residences, mess-room, kitchen, saddle and harness rooms, and immediately opposite this, the coach-house, with lofts over. On either side, in the semicircular parts, are stalls and boxes, with a place for cleaning in the centre of each.

A special feature in this design is the continuous covered-way all round the circle, forming an exercising ground for the animals as well as protection from weather.

The buildings are of red bricks and stone dressings, and red tiles for the roof; and this is broken up and varied by introducing some effective bits of half-timber work of quaint forms, being an inexpensive method of gaining variety, lightness, and colour. The accommodation here is for thirty-six horses.

The cost of this design would be about £6500. This estimate may seem inconsistent compared with some other examples in this book, which it will be observed are of a more elaborate character. This design has been prepared almost wholly with regard to economy of space and means, with little or no regard to architectural display.

DESIGN FOR STABLES FOR 36 HORSES .

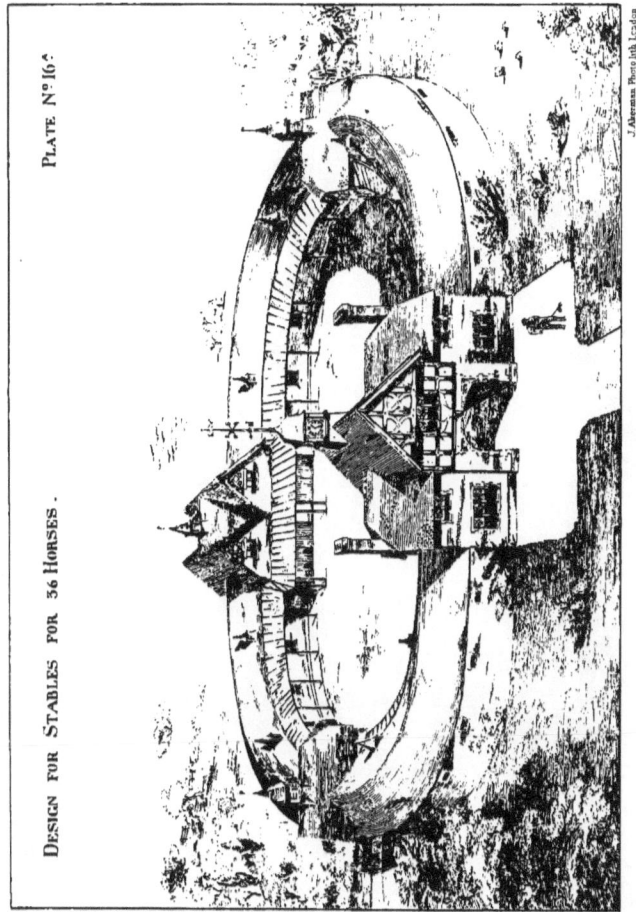

BIRDSEYE VIEW

THE STABLES · INGESTRE HALL · STAFFORDSHIRE

PLATE N? 19

IN QUADRANGLE LOOKING TOWARDS THE ENTRANCE

J. Akerman, Photo-lith. London

THE STABLES · INGESTRE HALL · STAFFORDSHIRE.

IN QUADRANGLE LOOKING TOWARDS CLOCK TOWER

PLATE Nº 17

NEW STABLES.
INGESTRE HALL

47

PLATES XVII., XVIII., & XIX.

The New Stables, Ingestre, Staffordshire.

THE stables at Ingestre Hall, Staffordshire, were built a few years
ago, from designs by the author, forming one of the largest
establishments in the country. The quadrangle is about 160 feet by
140 feet, and is approached through the archway in the centre, over
which rises a tower. On either side of the archway are residences for
coachmen and grooms, sick-boxes, and harness-rooms; and over the
latter are the granaries with fire-proof floors. The wings to the right
and left are the stables for stalls and loose-boxes, each wing having
a cleaning-place in the centre. These stables are built open half-way
up the roof, and ceiled with a panelled and plastered ceiling. The
ventilation and drainage was specially considered, and the most perfect
modern methods adopted, and all the fittings were of the most durable
and best kind. The coach-house occupies the central position of
quadrangle, and is of spacious dimensions, having a portico in front
for washing purposes, built of stone, with an elaborate oak clock-
turret on roof. Over the coach-house are found the hay and straw
lofts, helpers' rooms, &c. The mess-room, kitchen, forge, &c., are
built to the rear of this.

In designing this building no trouble was spared in rendering it
complete in all its arrangements and details, water and electric light
being taken into the stables and otherwise where necessary. The new
building is made to harmonise in style and feeling with the old Hall—
which was restored by the author at the same time—is built of brick
and stone, the entrance-tower and archway being entirely of the latter
material. Plate XVII. shows a bird's-eye view looking into quadrangle, with the façade towards the road. Plate XVIII. is the view
in quadrangle facing the coach-house; and Plate XIX. is a similar
one looking at the entrance to quadrangle.

The total cost of these stables was about £18,000, and the accommodation is for over fifty horses.

EXAMPLE OF A HUNTING-BOX.

PLATE XX.

View from the South-east.

HAVING endeavoured to show several grades of stable offices suited to the requirements of various descriptions of country houses, from the hunting-box or parsonage to the mansion, it may be appropriate to add to this little work a well-digested and attractive idea for a small residence, where a gentleman may retire for the hunting season and entertain a few friends comfortably. The view shown by Plate XX. is taken from the south-east or garden front, the house being intended to be entered from the north, and placed on the ground as near as possible due north and south, in order to secure as much sun to the reception-rooms and principal bedrooms as practicable. The author's idea of such a place is that it should be a gentleman's house in miniature, well and comfortably planned, possessing on a small scale all the arrangements and conveniences of a well-appointed establishment, while requiring only the minimum number of domestics to keep it in proper working order.

This design is based on a plan the author has used successfully in several instances, with certain modifications to suit the circumstances, and lately in Dorset, where it has given much satisfaction as a comfortable and attractive house. The plan might be still further improved on, for there is no standard of perfection: one can only judge from experience whether a house is really comfortable and well planned. The accommodation on the ground-plan would be a porch, an entrance-hall, to be used as a sitting-room, lavatory, gentlemen's

PLATE Nº 20

DESIGN FOR A HUNTING BOX

VIEW FROM THE SOUTH EAST

J. Akerman, Photo-lith, London

w.-c., and cloak-room, morning-room, drawing-room, dining-room, servants' hall, pantry, backstairs, kitchen, scullery, with the usual offices and some cellarage in basement. The chamber-floor would contain about seven or eight bedrooms and dressing-rooms, bath-room, water-closet, and housemaid's closet, and three or four servants' bedrooms.

The author considers a house of this description, including stabling for four or five horses, might be built for £3300 or thereabouts. There would appear to be a want of houses of this kind in good hunting localities. Noblemen and large landed proprietors, whether or not Masters of Hounds, would find this a fair investment, as such a house would command a good tenant on lease at a remunerative rent. Spare cash might be invested to much less advantage.

50

PLATE XXI.

View of Entrance Front.

THIS view shows the north or entrance front of the hunting-box, of which the last plate, No. XX., represents the south or garden front. The author has endeavoured to break up the façade as much as possible without detriment to the comfort of the interior, and has introduced a few quaint old-fashioned points peculiar to this style of architecture. The entrance-porch, with its half-timbered gable, the turret staircase at the side, and the bold old-fashioned chimney, form the main features of this façade, and mark the entrance to the house. The servants' offices are on the left-hand side towards the east, with the stables beyond. The north or entrance front would have a fore-court, with the gardens and pleasure-grounds on the south and west.

It will be observed, the disposition of this plan affords a pleasing and picturesque sky-line from almost every point of sight.

PLATE N.º21

DESIGN FOR HUNTING BOX
ENTRANCE FRONT

· HUNTING KENNEL · DESIGN A ·

PLATE Nº 25

J. Akerman. Photo. lith. London

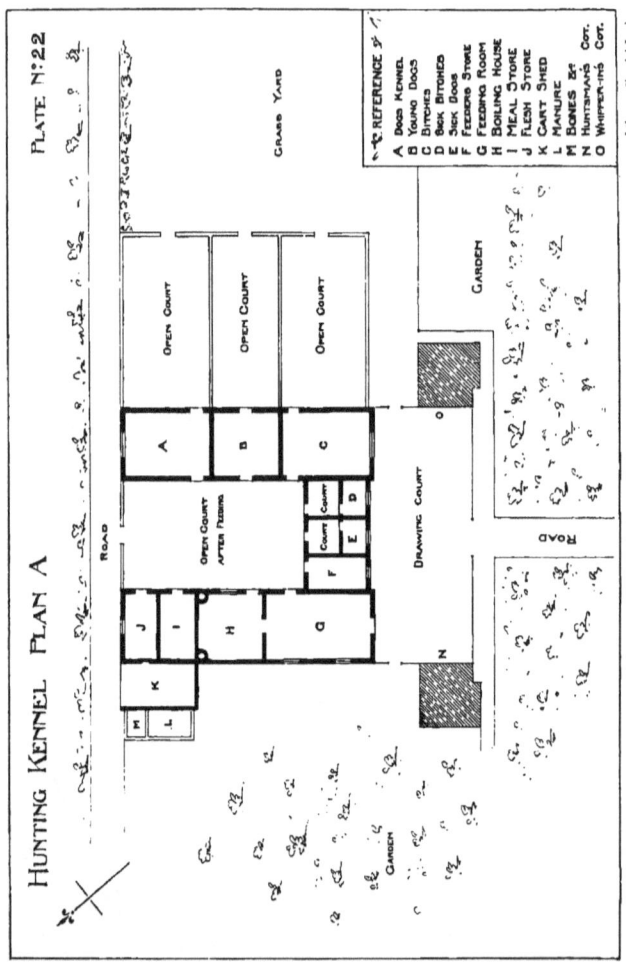

HUNTING KENNEL PLAN A

PLATE Nº 22

REFERENCE
A Dogs Kennel
B Young Dogs
C Bitches
D Sick Bitches
E Sick Dogs
F Feeding Store
G Feeding Room
H Boiling House
I Meal Store
J Flesh Store
K Cart Shed
L Manure
M Bones &c
N Huntsman's Cot.
O Whipper-in's Cot.

EXAMPLES OF HUNTING-KENNELS.

PLATES XXII. & XXIII.

Designs for Kennels, with Huntsman's Residence, &c.

THE favour with which the old English sport of fox-hunting is regarded in this country will be in itself a justification for the insertion of this design for a kennel, as much as the close connection there is between it and the subject of stables. Where a lodging for hounds has to be provided, it is as wise and economical in the long-run to have it well done at first, both with regard to the expenditure incurred in maintaining a building of any kind afterwards, and also as to the health and preservation of the animals, which must always necessarily be to some extent affected for good or for bad by the lodging into which they are introduced or in which they have been brought up. For instance, in the choice of a site one cannot be too fastidious, for in the proper selection of this depends to a great extent the comfort of the hounds, and their fit condition for the chase when required. At one time to such an extent had kennel-lameness grown amongst the various packs through out the country, that sporting gentlemen were at their wits' end to find out the reason why such an unfortunate disease was so rife. It has, however, now been fully explained, that anything in the shape of damp under or even surrounding a kennel, has a great deal to do with the outbreak of lameness. Therefore it is necessary that great care should be taken in the selection of a site, where the hounds have to spend a considerable part of their existence. Having decided upon a place where the soil is of a sufficiently dry and clayey nature, and if possible on the crest of some rising ground, it is necessary that the whole area of the building should be covered with at least six inches of Portland cement concrete on a bed of dry brick-rubbish, which, though not under every circumstance quite impervious to damp, would be sufficiently so where the site is carefully selected. This I consider one of the most essential points to be aimed at in the construction of kennels. Allied to this is, of course, the proper drainage of the site and building. If the kennel is placed on a rising ground, the wet will to a large extent percolate away from it; but in addition to this natural advantage, it will be found of the utmost benefit to lay an ordinary field-drain, with open joints and overflows leading away from the kennel, to assist the natural process, and more speedily clear the precincts of the surface-water. By these means an area of a perfectly dry nature will be acquired, and a perfectly safe place to raise your building for the lodging of the hounds and other accessories.

The arrangement of the several parts of the building now come under our notice, and although I have found many examples throughout the country that have been very well arranged, yet I do not think it will be presumptuous to add the two examples which I have endeavoured to convey to the mind of the reader in Plates XXII., XXIII., and XXIV., XXV. Plate XXII. shows a plan to the accompanying view, XXIII., of a small kennel to accommodate, say, a three days' pack. The first requirement to be considered is the aspect to which the kennels will be exposed, and I have laid them down facing the south-east. This gives the sun to the dogs in the early morning and throughout the best part of the day, up to a time when it may get too strong and warm for keeping them in good condition,—I fancy too much sun in summer is as bad as too little. One end of this wing is reserved for the dogs, while the other is for bitches, and the chamber between the two lodges the young hounds. There would thus be little quarrelling among the dogs, being placed at a sufficient distance from the others. To each chamber is put a court with enclosing walls of height enough to prevent the dogs annoying each other, surmounted with an iron railing about eight feet high. On the south-west front a drawing-court might or might not be put, according to the judgment of the owner, who might wish to occasionally show the pack. In any case, it would be useful for drawing before feeding. In the wing to the north-west has been contrived the feeding-chamber with its usual accessories—a boiling-house and flesh and meal store. By this arrangement the hounds can be taken in from the drawing-court and fed, then turned into the after-feeding court, from whence they would be led to their separate lodgings. The boiling-house adjoins the feeding-chamber, but would be effectually cut off from it and the meal-store, and properly ventilated by flues through the roof. In the centre wing, towards the south-west, is a room for the feeder, a room for drying purposes, and a hospital. This completes the accommodation of a small kennel; and if it is found desirable to place the huntsman and whipper-in near to them, they might be placed as indicated on the plan. Provision should be made in the courts for troughs, so arranged that the animals will not be able to foul the drinking-water.

The floor of the kennels is best of Portland cement concrete, laid with proper falls and channels to the drains, taken outside and thoroughly disconnected and trapped. Arrangements could be contrived for utilising the heat of the boiling-house, and conveying it across to the kennel in cold weather by means of a conduit running under the court, and a hot-water or hot-air coil in each chamber; but this would not be often necessary, as the dogs would keep each other warm enough if the rooms are not made too large. In the ceiling of each lodging there would be an opening about eighteen inches square, with a hinged flap, and cords to open and shut at pleasure. The vitiated air would pass through this opening into the roof, and be sucked away by the ventilator on the ridge.

Although it is not desirable that a great deal of expense be put on the exterior of the kennels, yet every gentleman will see the desirability of making it in harmony with the other buildings on his estate, and the eye will not be offended by the judicious introduction of a few ornamental features; but this ought to be kept in subjection to the more needful things which conduce to the comfort and health of the occupants, which, after having been attained, can be added to and enhanced according to the taste and discretion of the person interested.

54

PLATES XXIV. & XXV.

Design for Kennels, &c.

WE now come to the consideration of kennels on a more extended
scale than that just brought under our notice in the last Plate.
Without presuming to any practical knowledge as to the proper management of hounds, it lies quite within my province to make suggestions
and remarks as to the housing of these animals, and the best method of
arranging their quarters in regard to their health and management.

As I have already said, the principal and most important points
which should guide one in the erection of kennels is, first, the selection
of a proper site on a soil that is naturally dry and unabsorbent, free
and open to the air. Having gained that point, it is then necessary
that the aspect be studied, and all other matters of arrangement and
detail should follow and fall in with these in the manner found to be
most convenient. Plan B shows a method of arrangement which
would work well where a large establishment was kept up. In this
plan there is a kennel for a hunting-pack and another for a resting-
pack. The kennel for the hunting-pack faces the south-east, and
derives all the benefit to be had from the sun from early morn till
mid-day. There is a lodging for dogs and young hounds, and each is
provided with a court enclosed with walls and iron railing. In the
opposite wing are the quarters for the resting-pack, and at the extreme
end of the wing, as far as possible from the neighbourhood of the dogs,
is accommodation for bitches. Each of these also has a court in front,
and the aspect is towards the north-west. The floors of these chambers,
as well as the rest of the buildings, would be paved with Portland
cement concrete, and the cement rendering carried up for about three
feet above the floor as a precaution against any chances of damp being
sucked through the walls. The ventilation of the lodgings would be

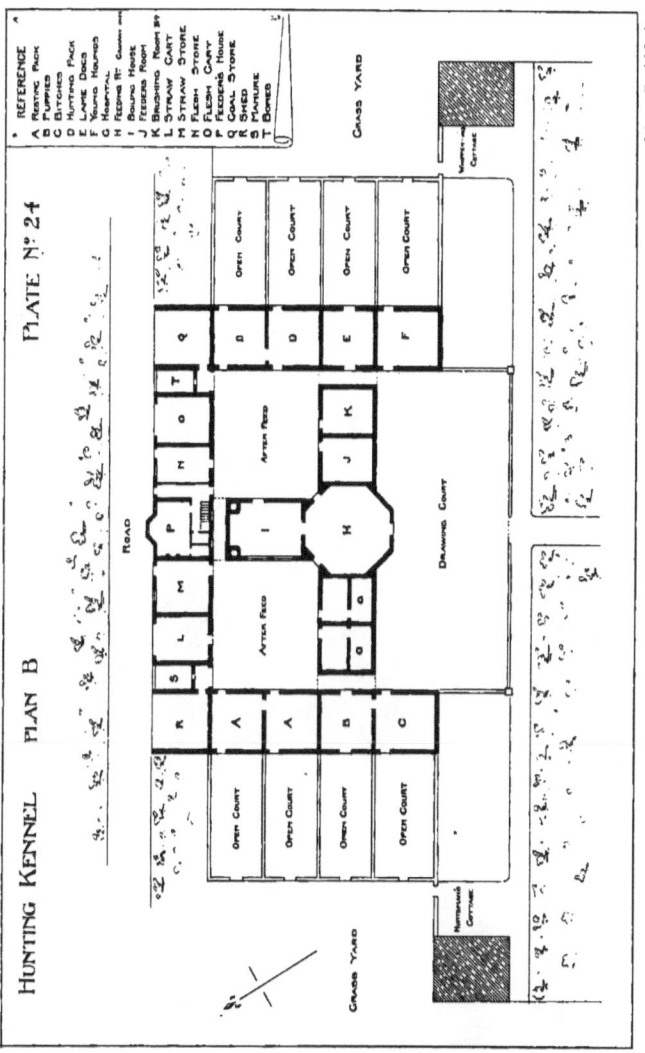

HUNTING KENNEL   PLAN B   PLATE Nº 24

REFERENCE
A RESTING PACK
B PUPPIES
C BITCHES
D HUNTING PACK
E LAME DOGS
F YOUNG HOUNDS
G HOSPITAL
H FEEDING ST GROOMING
I BOILING HOUSE
J FEEDERS ROOM
K BREEDING ROOM BY
L STRAW CART
M STRAW STORE
N FLESH STORE
O FLESH CART
P FEEDERS HOUSE
Q COAL STORE
R SHED
S MANURE
T BONES

GRASS YARD

ROAD

J. Akerman Photo Litho London

HUNTING KENNEL · DESIGN B ·

PLATE N° 25

J. Akerman. Photo-lith London

carried out by the admission of fresh air from the windows; and the
foul air would be carried off by the ventilation openings in the ceiling,
and thence through the ventilators on the ridge. By these means a
continuous current of fresh air would be passing through the room,
and keeping the atmosphere sweet and clean without lowering the
temperature. The kennels might be warmed in a most effectual, and,
at the same time, in a most economical way, by putting a small gas
furnace in each shed adjoining the dogs' lodging, and carrying a flow
and return pipe through the kennels. This would make up for any
deficiency of warmth, and equalise the temperature in very cold weather,
as it is only in very cold weather that it would be necessary to use
this. The heat derived from this source would do a great deal towards
drying and dispelling damp that by any accident might arise.

Having lodged your hounds, the next requirement is to feed them.
The feeding-room has been placed in the centre of the building, as
being the most easily accessible of all positions, and the best for dis-
tribution, as will be seen. This place would serve for both packs,
would be comparatively lofty and open up to the roof, upon which
would be placed a ventilator for the purpose of carrying off the steam
arising from the pudding, &c. In front of the feeding-house is the
drawing-court, where the hounds may whet their appetites before
being taken into the feeding-room, and where they can be drawn
previous to the day's work, or for purposes of inspection. From the
feeding-house are two doorways leading each into an after-feeding
court, one of these belonging to each pack, so that as much quiet as
possible may be enjoyed by the working-pack. Entrance to the
kennels is provided from these courts. Adjoining the feeding-room
is the boiling-house, with meal and flesh boilers and other adjuncts to
this room, and overhead in the roof is a meal-store with meal-shoot to
boiler. The steam which would otherwise arise in this room is carried
off by a separate flue from the furnace, with proper zinc hoods.
Within easy reach of the boiling-house is the flesh-store, with an
adjoining room for the flesh-cart, a coal-store, and manure-pit for
bones, &c. In the centre of the back wing is the residence for feeder,
containing living-room, scullery, and pantry, and two bedrooms on
the chamber-floor, having easy access to the courts and kennels when
necessary. To the left of this are found the straw-store, a place for
straw-cart and a manure-pit; and at each extreme end or corner an
open shed for the sheltering of stray hounds. On the left of the

feeding-room are the hospitals for dogs and bitches, and on the other side a room for the feeder and a drying-room. The bath I should have placed at a short distance from the kennels, and if possible in running water; but I should lay on as much water as I could to the courts and kennels for drinking and working purposes, for this is very essential to the cleanliness and sweetness of the establishment, and a great saving of time and labour. There should be drinking-troughs in each yard and court, taps in the boiling-house and feeding-room, and elsewhere. All the rain-water from the roofs should be conducted along the guttering to a rain-water tank, and used in feeding the drinking-troughs in the courts, &c.

I will not say anything as to the drainage, as the nature of the site would in each case have something to do with the arrangement of the drains; but in all cases in the building I would recommend open drains, so far as practicable. The drains outside the building ought to be cut off altogether from any connection with the inside, trapped and ventilated according to the most approved principles of modern times.

The bird's-eye view shown on Plate XXV. will give a very tolerable idea of the disposition of the principal parts of the building. The two side-wings with their yards are devoted to the accommodation of the hounds, the back-wing is taken up with feeder's house, stores, and sheds, while the centre block is occupied by the feeding department. I have attempted to give some little architectural pretensions to the front of this building by receding in the space between the two side-wings, and marking the centre by slightly elevating the roof and crowning it with a ventilator. The gable-ends of side-wings have been treated with a plain design of half-timbering and projecting gables. The buildings would be built of brick with tiled roofs, and the whole would doubtless present a pleasing aspect to the eye. Residences for the huntsmen and whippers-in might be provided where shown on the plan, also stabling for hacks and cart-horses in some convenient site near to the kennels.

EXAMPLE OF WOODEN LOOSE BOXES IN A PADDOCK

PLATE N.° 26

EXAMPLE OF LOOSE-BOXES FOR SUMMERING HORSES.

PLATE XXVI.

LOOSE-BOXES built of wood are useful for stabling hunters in summer, and for brood-mares or stallions. These should be placed in a well-sheltered situation, with a south-east aspect; and in order to keep the yards dry, the ground should gradually slope from the boxes and be further dealt with as hereafter described. Another form of plan, say for four or six boxes, would be to place the fodder-store in the centre of the block, by which plan the yards might be made wider than the boxes, and some symmetrical form of plan obtained. The rain-water from the roof ought to be conserved and stored in rain-water butts, and it would be well to have two water-butts connected together, the first one partly filled with fine sand and gravel for filtering purposes. The boxes hereafter described are of a superior character, as will be gathered from the description. Of course it is possible to erect less expensive loose-boxes, which perhaps would answer every purpose, for about the rate of two pounds sterling for every superficial yard of space the boxes cover, and this price would include the cost of yards and fodder-houses.

This plate shows a range of loose-boxes recently erected by the author for a nobleman in Surrey, in a paddock adjoining his mansion. They consist of three boxes and a fodder-store. The boxes are each 14 feet by 14 feet, and are wholly constructed of timber-framing and weather-boarding, on sound brick and concrete foundations. The roof is boarded and slated. The divisions of boxes, and the walls round boxes to the same height, are lined with deal boarding stained and varnished, finished on the top with an oak capping. The corn-troughs or mangers are lined down to the floor to prevent the horses injuring their knees. The ventilation and drainage of these boxes have been carried out in a simple but effective manner, the fresh air being admitted from an opening above the heads of the horses, with louvre-frame and close-fitting flap to open and close when required. The upper parts of windows are also hung to open inwards, admitting fresh air. The foul air is carried up to ceiling by the upward current and taken off by the ventilation openings in ceiling, which are also constructed so as to open and close at pleasure when the temperature requires to be regulated. The floors are formed of Wilkinson's granitic paving, laid with a fall towards the door, and discharging into an open gully-trap outside, thereby effectually cutting off all risk of effluvia arising in the boxes from the drains. To each loose-box there is a grass-yard attached, enclosed with a high oak pale-fence, with doors opening out to the paddock. At one end of the building is the fodder-store, of sufficient size to supply the number of boxes.

This is less expensive than a brick building (though perhaps not so durable), and was erected complete at the cost of £250, including the grass-yard enclosures.

VIEW OF HUNTING STABLE

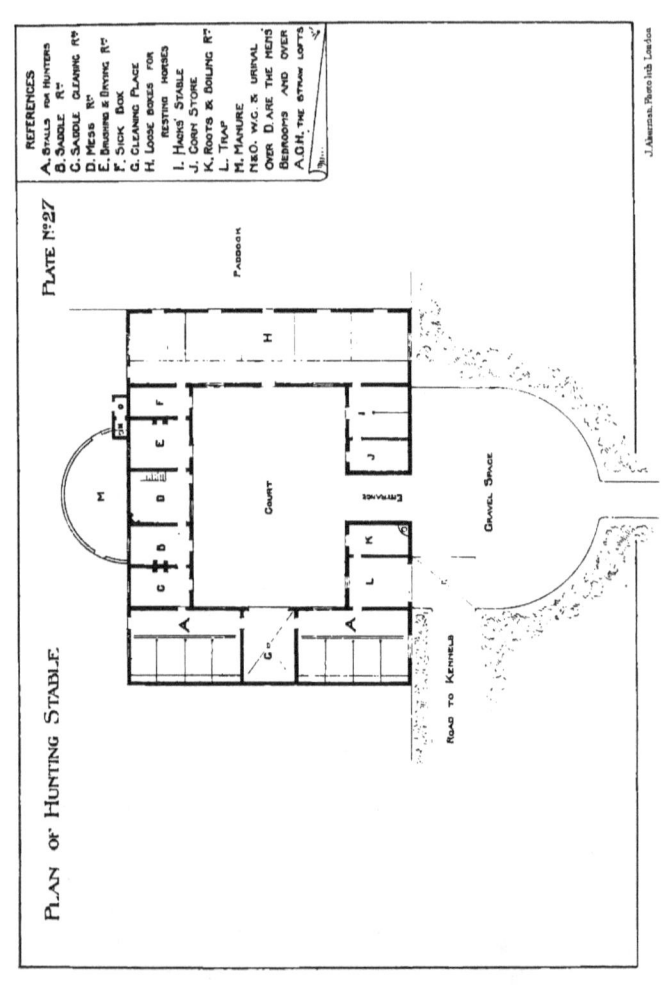

PLAN OF HUNTING STABLE

PLATE Nº27

REFERENCES
A. STALLS for HUNTERS
B. SADDLE Rᵐ
C. SADDLE CLEANING Rᵐ
D. MESS Rᵐ
E. BRUSHING & DRYING Rᵐ
F. SICK BOX
G. CLEANING PLACE
H. LOOSE BOXES FOR RESTING HORSES
I. HACKS STABLE
J. CORN STORE
K. ROOTS & BOILING Rᵐ
L. TRAP
M. MANURE
N&O. W.C. & URINAL OVER D ARE THE MENS BEDROOMS AND OVER A.G.H. THE STRAW LOFTS

PADDOCK

COURT

ENTRANCE

GRAVEL SPACE

ROAD TO KENNELS

J. Akerman. Photo lith London

EXAMPLE OF A HUNTING-STABLE.

A HUNTING-STABLE differs in many respects from the ordinary stables attached to a country house, and a building for this purpose must be specially planned in order to meet the necessary requirements. In placing before the reader this example for the accommodation of a small hunting-stud, my object is not so much to show the features of a permanent building, but rather to furnish a design of stabling, &c., for a moderate number of horses such as might be expected to accompany the example of the hunting-box illustrated on Plates XX. and XXI., laid down on the lines of the strictest economy, and made a separate building altogether from the stable which would necessarily be attached to the house. The accommodation provided is for eight hunting and five resting horses. There is also a stable for two hacks, making a total of fifteen horses. The stall-stables, A, are placed on the left hand as you enter the courtyard, and the boxes, II, on the right, facing and opening out towards the south, so as to get as much sun as possible. There is a coach-house, I., entered from the outside of the building, so that no vehicles enter the courtyard, which is left undisturbed to the men and horses. In the centre, between the stall-stables, is a cleaning-place for the horses, from which each stall-stable is entered. At one end, adjoining and communicating with the stable, is the room, C, for cleaning saddles, &c. ; and the next room, D, is for hanging same and a mess-room. There is also a brushing and drying room with fireplace and stove, sick-box, root and boiling house and corn-store; and sleeping accommodation is found for the men-servants over the mess-room, D. In the roof over the stables and boxes are spaces for hay and straw respectively.

The construction of the front wall of building would be of half-timber framing, filled in with brickwork. All the remaining walls would be of timber and weather-boarding, on brick and concrete foundations. The roofs tiled or slated on boarding, and the boxes lined out with wood, ventilated and drained· similar to what has already been described for the boxes of Plate XXVI.

The cost of this would probably be £1000.

DESIGN FOR A TRAINING
ESTABLISHMENT

PLATE Nº 50

INDEX

A STABLE YARD
B ENTRANCE
C EXERCISING YARD
D ENTRANCE TO DO.
E LOOSE BOXES
F STALL STABLE
G SADDLE ROOMS
H SITTING RM & DORMITORY
  FOR LADS
I TRAINERS HOUSE
J BUSINESS ENTRANCE
K TRADESMENS' ENTRANCE
L LAWN
M GARDEN
N KITCHEN GARDEN
O PADDOCK
P WORKING YARD
Q HEAD LADS COTTAGE
R GARDEN
S WATER TOWER
T PUBLIC ROAD

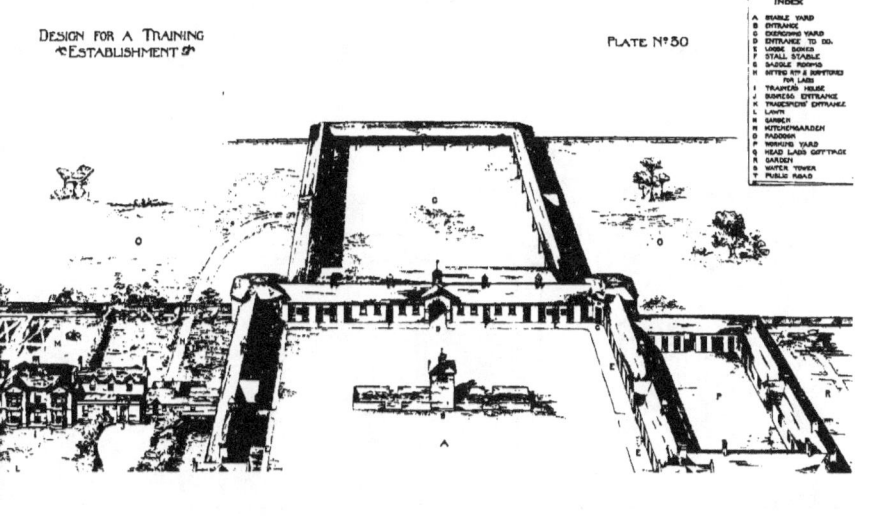

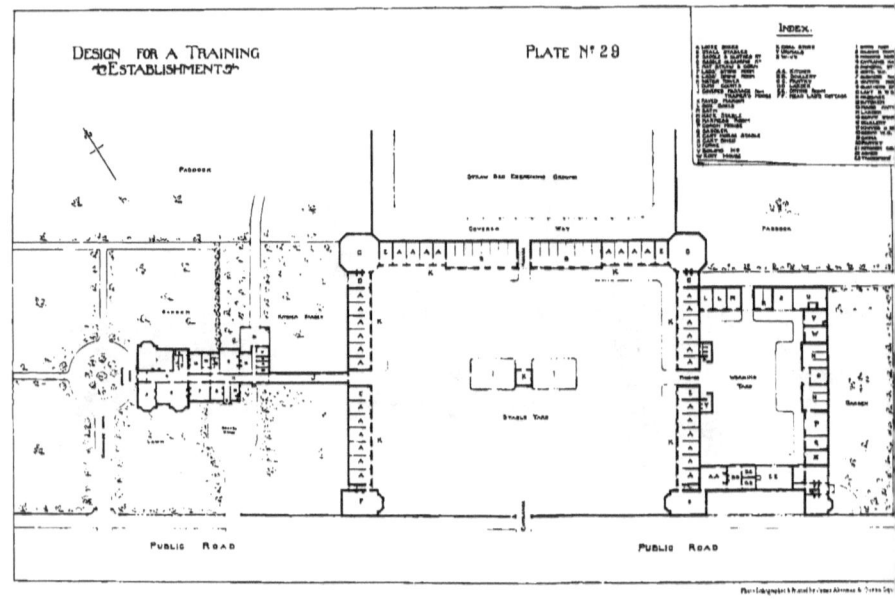

DESIGN FOR A TRAINING ⚜ESTABLISHMENT⚜

PLATE Nº 29

PUBLIC ROAD

PUBLIC ROAD

EXAMPLE

OF A

TRAINING ESTABLISHMENT TO ACCOMMODATE FIFTY HORSES.

— ◆ —

PLATES XXIX. & XXX.

SOME years ago, at the request of a much-respected and distinguished member of the Jockey Club, I had occasion to inspect in a professional capacity the principal racing establishments at Newmarket. Some time was spent looking over five or six stables, and the buildings that pleased me most were those built for the late Mr Joseph Dawson, and designed, I believe, by the late racing judge, Mr J. F. Clark. At that time these stables were considered the best. Built in the Italian style of architecture, with, if I remember rightly, a very comfortable trainer's house, the long façade of the stables was broken up by a tower. The planning of the boxes, the arrangements for fodder and other details of comfort and convenience for carrying on the business of so large an establishment, were points in the buildings which the late Mr Dawson took especial pleasure in explaining to his friends; and I still possess a lively recollection of the hospitality and kindness I met with. The example which the readers are invited to study has been prepared with great care, and contains such arrangements and conveniences conceived to be necessary for an establishment of this kind. The plan has been carefully considered by a gentleman

i

eminently qualified to form an opinion, who considers it admirable, and on which he could not suggest any alteration. With these few preliminary remarks I now proceed to explain the plan, and point out what may be considered its merits.

In describing the arrangement of this example, I have endeavoured to elucidate the different positions of the several parts, by presenting a bird's-eye view with letters and an index, so that the arrangement may be more readily apprehended than would probably be the case with the geometrical drawing.

The primary requirements in planning an establishment like this are such as may secure the greatest comfort to the horses, combined with cleanliness, health, and quietness ; and these are the considerations which have guided me in the conception and working out of this idea.

The stable-yard is entered from the public road by a gate in the centre. This yard is of liberal dimensions, as will be seen, and is surrounded on three sides chiefly by loose-boxes, with a stall-stable in the centre.

Each stable or chamber contains some six and some four loose-boxes, the divisions of which are about 7 ft. high, finished with a ventilating rail above this height. Above this the chamber or stable is open to the ceiling from end to end. Each division also has a sliding door in it, so that the tour of the stables may be made, if necessary, under cover. These boxes have been so placed as to secure the maximum amount of sunshine, so far as a symmetrical arrangement of the plan would afford. The ventilation of these boxes and stalls would be similar to what has already been described in the preceding examples.

At the two most central points of the building, marked G in the bird's-eye view, the saddle-rooms have been placed, access to which can be had from any of the boxes without having to go outside. These rooms are made large, as they also serve for storing dry horse-clothing. Adjoining each saddle-room, and communicating with it, is the necessary adjunct of cleaning-chamber for saddles, &c., with sinks and water, and other necessaries. Within easy distance of each stable several rooms have been distributed for hay, straw, and corn ; and I have thought this preferable to making one large chamber for the storage of same, as in the former case small quantities for each section are so frequently replenished that they do not suffer deterioration in rotting or being fouled. In addition to this, of course, sufficient storage might be provided for in the adjoining paddocks to last for any length of time.

The sitting-room and dormitories for lads are placed at the ends of each side-wing. The dormitories over the lads' sitting-room and dining-room would be each divided into ten cubicals to each chamber, and it would be easy to find additional room if required.

In the centre of the yard a water-tower would be necessary to distribute water throughout, and on either side of this structure the dung-courts have been provided for. The rain-water that would fall upon the roofs would be considerable, and this I would collect and conserve in built rain-water tanks, and pump the same when necessary into the tanks in tower, where separate tanks would be provided, one for hard and one for soft water—the latter to be used for drinking purposes.

In the centre of the right wing is an arched passage which leads to the working-court. The buildings in this portion of the design are so placed that all noise and bustle inseparable from a large establishment may be excluded from the principal court where the racing-horses are housed, and so ensure them the quiet they need. Here are stables for six hacks and two cart-horses, coach-house, harness-room, cart-shed, forge, boiling and root houses, coal-store, and conveniences for men. There is also a cart entrance from the side road to this court.

The advantage of placing the supernumerary portion of the establishment outside the stable-yard in a quadrangle of its own must strike one as evident enough, besides being a great help to order and cleanliness. All the work outside the actual attendance and grooming can be carried on here away from view; and visitors would not be offended by the hundred-and-one sounds which usually assail one on entering, when all these things are hopelessly mixed up, without any regard to a proper arrangement of plan.

Attached to the dining-room, and forming the south wing of this court, is the kitchen department for the lads, comprising kitchen, scullery, pantry, and larder, and if necessary, accommodation for two female servants over them. There is also a drying-room for horse-clothes, &c.; and in the corner next this a cottage residence, which the head lad, as a married man—under the trainer—would occupy.

In the rear of the stable-yard, and approached by a passage in the centre of the building, is a straw-bed exercising-ground of ample dimensions, surrounded by a covered riding-way, to be used in wet weather. From this are two exits to the paddocks, marked O in view.

From the wing on the left of the stable-yard is a covered passage leading to the trainer's house, so that patrons can inspect the stables in any weather. To this house I have provided an entrance for business purposes, marked J, and a separate and private entrance for the inhabitants and others. The trainer will thus be able to enjoy the privacy of his own dwelling and grounds apart from the interruptions of business. The accommodation provided in the residence is as indicated on the plan by the numeral letters, with a comfortable and well-planned set of bed-chambers on the one-pair floor.

It is to be noted with what facility the trainer may be able to inspect and show his stud. As the horses are usually tied up, it is possible to pass from the business-room in the trainer's house along the covered way, and from loose-box to loose-box, &c., through the sliding doors, until he has made a complete inspection, and then return to his business-room, without being unnecessarily exposed to the elements.

The style of treatment adopted for the exterior is admirably suited to buildings of this kind, where economy has to be much considered without sacrificing them altogether to ugliness. The walls might be built of red brick or stone, and the roofs boarded and slated. All the roofs would be low-pitched and in harmony with the style, and for economical reasons.

In some of the loose-boxes there ought to be provision for benches on which to sleep, for lads who are put in charge of certain horses— and I think one such arrangement should be put in each stable ; but best of all is a portable bench, which can be placed in any box at pleasure at any time.